CYRIL THE LION

Text by Emma Mora

Illustrations by Kennedy

Translation by Jean Grasso Fitzpatrick

BARRON'S

Woodbury, New York/London/Toronto/Sydney

CYRIL THE LION AND HIS FRIENDS

Cyril the lion, hero of our tale,
Was a hundred years old and rather frail.
His mane was mangy and so thin it's sad,
And his tail full of knots looked just as bad.
The muscles that were once so strong
Now drooped and sagged as he walked along.
If that weren't enough to make him feel bad,
He'd lost every tooth he ever had!
He couldn't hunt either, sad to say—
Catching three flies took him half the day.

And what did Cyril like to eat?
Not zebra, gazelle, or any kind of meat,
Or the other foods that young lions munch.
It was oatmeal that Cyril had for lunch!
He loved bananas without the peel,
Then had milk through a straw for his evening meal.

There wasn't an animal, big or small,
Who was afraid of our friend Cyril at all.
They were calm and happy, and do you know why?
Because Cyril the lion wouldn't hurt a fly!
He had even made friends with two or three
Who were his enemies—or used to be.

But then one day
A dentist came along.
He carried a small bag
And sang a happy song.
Cyril didn't think twice
About asking his advice.
"I may be the King
Of the Jungle," he said,
"But I don't impress anyone
Without a tooth in my head.

"Since you're an expert
In dentistry
Could you please make
Some dentures for me?"
The dentist was kind
And said he wouldn't mind.

He listened to Cyril's
Heart for a while.
"It's beating just fine,"
He said with a smile.

Then he looked
At Cyril's nose,
At his eyes,
And at his toes.

He counted Cyril's whiskers.
It didn't take long.
None of them was missing
And they were curly and strong.

He examined Cyril
From head to toe,
Then untied his tail—
"No extra charge, you know!

"Now Cyril, will you cough for me?
Please say 'aah' so I can see.

"That's good, Cyril.
Now open wide,
So I can have a look inside!

"What's this I see?
Now that's too bad!
Where are all
The teeth you had?
My goodness, this
Is very sad!

"If you had remembered to do just one thing,
My dear but toothless Jungle King,
And brushed your teeth after every meal,
No matter how lazy or tired you feel,
Well, Cyril, then, I must confess,
You'd never have ended in this mess."

Now when Cyril heard
What the dentist had to say
He felt so awful
He nearly fainted away.
The dentist scratched his head
And cheerfully said—

"Your Highness, is this any way
For a King to act? Oh, no, I say.
Even if your royal mouth is a mess,
I'll make it good as new—more or less.
Now give me a nice big smile, I say,
Or I'll pack my bag and go away."

"Oh, please don't go, we aren't yet through!
I'll try my best to smile at you.
Now measure my jaw and measure my head,
And I'll follow your advice," Cyril said.

When the good dentist
Had looked Cyril over,
He tickled his armpits
With a sprig of clover.
Then he measured
His jaw and his head.
"Do you sleep through the winter?"
He absent-mindedly said.

Now, when Cyril heard the dentist say that,
He became a very angry cat.
He leaped to his feet, looking fierce and proud,
And scared the dentist, his roar was so loud!
"But who do you think I am?" said he.
"Mr. Dentist, you've offended me!
I'm not a lazy-bones, like a bear
I haven't slept since late last year.
Lions do not hibernate!
Now let's be sure to get that straight!
If you want a life that's long and happy,
Make me some dentures—and make it snappy."

The dentist was so frightened that his knees began to shake.
"I'm sorry, sir," he stammered, "I made a big mistake!
I know that you're a lion—who could think otherwise?
I'll make sure that your dentures are the perfect size!"

By the time another month passed by
Cyril was feeling lively and spry.
His new teeth looked so sharp and strong
As he smiled at everyone all day long.
But the animals worried when he came out of his den:
Did this mean Cyril would start hunting them again?

But though Cyril the lion
Felt strong as iron,

His favorite foods
On which to sup
Were still milk and oatmeal—
They filled him up!

He just used his teeth to smile, like you!
Hunting wasn't something he wanted to do.
He liked to hunt in his younger days,
But now he preferred to sit and laze.

Now that Cyril
Looked like a king
He could command respect
Without doing a thing.
He didn't need a crown,
Or a robe, or a wreath.
No!—just a set of
New false teeth!

And every morning and every night,
He roared and roared with all his might.
But it wasn't meant to be at all scary
To any creature, feathered or hairy.
It just was Cyril's laughing way
Of announcing the start and end of each day.

ROVER, THE DOG WHO RULED THE HENHOUSE

Cockaroo the rooster, one sad day,
Stopped crowing, forever—what more can I say?
To tell the truth, the hens didn't cry—
For Cockaroo was a bossy kind of a guy.
Now the hens could do everything they couldn't do before:
Come and go when they pleased, eat, or drink, or snore.

Even Pina, who never, ever did a bad thing,
Put green dye on her tail and wing.
She had fights with the geese and was always making noise.
She sang, "What fun! Life's full of joys!"

The other hens would not be outdone.
They played all sorts of pranks—for spite and for fun.
They flew straight to the kitchen and up on the beds,
Right to the pigpen and on the pigs' heads!

They walked through the vineyard to stretch their legs.
They gobbled the grapes and quit laying eggs.

Mama hen didn't know what to do.
Even the chicks were doing tricks, too.
One climbed in the pail and refused to come out.
The others did nothing but laugh and shout.
And they all ran away—yes, all five!
"Oh, if only your father were still alive!"

The barnyard was in a dreadful uproar—
Nothing like this had ever happened before!
So Rover decided to set things right.
"Let's stop this nonsense, one-two-three!
I'm the boss now, hens, so listen to me!
Get back on your nests and lay some eggs,
And stay out of the vineyard when you stretch your legs!
Anyone who doesn't listen to me
Is going to be sorry—just wait and see!

"And that includes the little chicks, too.
If I bark, I don't want a peep out of you!
From now on I'm the king around here,
And you'd better obey me, is that clear?"

Tabby Cat smiled; she hadn't missed a thing.
"I'm safe," she said, "as long as Rover's king.
He'll be so busy with the chicks,
I'll be able to play all my tricks!
So let him be king! That's quite all right!
I'll give him a curtsy each morning and night!"